Bees in the City

Bees in the City

by
Andrea Cheng

illustrated by
Sarah McMenemy

TILBURY HOUSE PUBLISHERS
Thomaston, Maine

"Aunt Celine's honey is the best in the world," I say, licking the honey off my fingers.

Papa puts a spoonful of the golden honey into his tea. "That's because she has the best helper in the world."

"Who?" I ask.

"A beekeeper named Lionel," Papa says.

I run to answer the phone.

"Oh Lionel," Aunt Celine says. "I have bad news."

I imagine my aunt wearing her bee vale with a smoker in her hand. "Did you get stung?"

"Worse than that. Many of our bees died over the winter, and the ones that are left are weak."

"What happened?"

Aunt Celine explains that all around her farm there used to be gardens with corn and tomatoes and mustard. But now, there are only fields of wheat. "Bees don't like to eat the same thing day after day."

"What can we do?" I ask.

Aunt Celine sighs. "I don't know, Lionel."

When I hang up, I go out to the balcony
and look at the tall buildings all around.

Beyond them is the edge of Paris, and beyond that is Aunt Celine's farm. All winter I waited to help her work the honeybees. And now they might not survive.

I go down to the fifth floor to find Alice.
"My bees are weak," I tell her.

She pulls her eyebrows together. "Maybe
the warm sun will help." We play two
games of checkers but I lose both. Then we
go down to the fourth floor to find Samir.

"Let's play Dragon," he says, pretending to
breathe fire through his nostrils.

"Lionel's bees are weak," Alice tells him.

"Dragons will protect them," he says. We go
behind the sofa castle to fight for our bee
hives, but I cannot stop worrying.

Mama makes a salad for lunch. "Everything will be okay," she says, patting my head.

I see a bee hover over our lavender. Then it darts next door to Mrs. Li's lotus flower. An idea flies into my head so fast that I knock over my glass of milk on my way to the phone.

"I have the perfect place for our bees," I tell my aunt. "It has lots of different plants in a very small space."

"Where is that?"

"Our apartment building!"

"Of course," Aunt Celine says. "On the roof!"

In the afternoon, Alice and I visit the landlord, Mr. Dubi, in his office.

"We were wondering—" Alice says.

"If we can keep honeybees," I say.

"On the roof," Alice says.

Mr. Dubi considers. "If everyone in the building agrees, I will agree too."

"We have to do a survey," Samir says, sitting down at the computer.

Do you like honey? Please support our bees. They will live on the roof and get pollen from our balcony flowers. Check "Yes" if you agree.

We print a lot of copies and tape them onto the door of every apartment in our building.

Later we go door to door, collecting the surveys.

"Okay," Alice whispers, each time she sees the checked box.

Samir stops in front of apartment 23. "Not okay," he whispers.

Mr. LaRosa comes to the door. His eyes are red and he is holding a handkerchief to his nose. "I'm afraid honeybees may sting my grandchildren," he says.

"My bees are peaceful," I say.

"And honey is good for colds," Alice says.

Mr. Larosa coughs. "I need all the help I can get," he says.

I hold my breath.

He checks the box.

Alice and Samir have to go home. I sit on our balcony
waiting for the sun to set, because bees can only travel
in the dark.

Finally I see Aunt Celine's truck turn the corner.

We unstrap the hive and carry it carefully up the steps, all the way to the rooftop terrace.

Aunt Celine is in a hurry to get back to her farm.

"What should I do now?" I ask.

"Wait," she says. "Honeybees need time to get oriented."

I look out at all the lights of Paris. "I hope you will be happy here,"
I whisper to our bees before following my aunt down the stairs.

In the morning our bees are circling the hive, but they have no idea where to go.

"Our balcony has lavender," I say. The bees hover around me. "That way," I point.

But the bees do not understand.

Aunt Celine calls. "How are things?"

"Not so good," I say.

"Ignore them for a while," she suggests.

Alice, Samir, and I play a long game of Monopoly. I keep looking out at the flowers on our balcony, but I don't see any bees. Alice and Samir haven't seen any on their balconies either.

"Maybe they died," I say.

"Let's play Dragon," Samir says.

For over two hours we try to use our dragon powers to attract honeybees, but we still don't see any.

Mam, Papa, and I go to the beach for the weekend, and when we get back, Aunt Celine is waiting. She and I walk up the narrow steps to the rooftop. I hold my breath as Aunt Celine puffs the smoker and takes the top off the hive. Then I peer over the top. Our bees are moving in and out of their tiny cells!

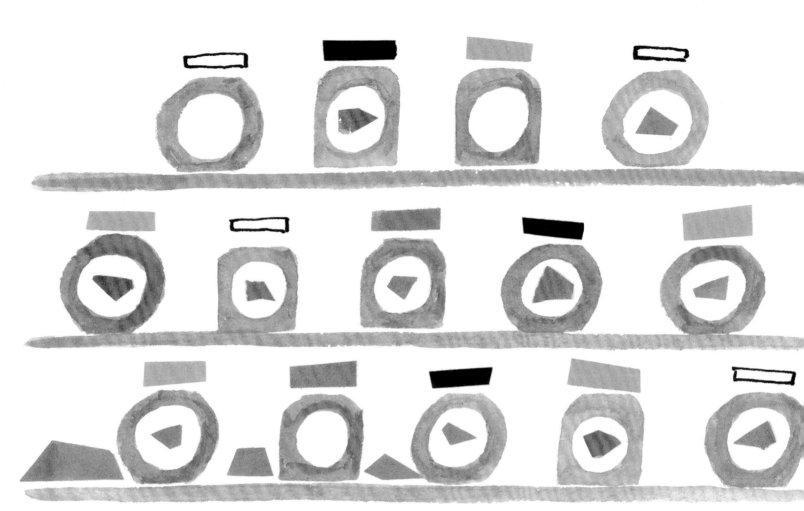

On Friday, we extract the honey and put it into jars in the basement.

"What should we call our honey?" Aunt Celine asks.

I know that honeybees don't fly far. But even on the balconies of our building there are so many kinds of flowers. "Around the World Honey," I say.

I draw a label with tall buildings. Alice and Samir add bees all around. Soon we have small jars of Around the World Honey for all of our neighbors.

Everyone in the building gathers in the courtyard to celebrate.

"I taste my lotus flower," Mrs. Li says.

"I taste our dill," Mr. Dubi says.

"Hurray for Around the World Honey," Mr. LaRosa shouts.

"Hurray for our healthy honeybees," I say, putting my arms around Alice and Samir.

HONEYBEES AND URBAN BEEKEEPING

Honeybees are amazing insects. Each one has five eyes and two pairs of wings that can beat 180 times per second. Honeybees live in colonies, or *hives*. Each hive has one queen bee who lays about 1,500 eggs per day in the summer. There are 40,000 to 60,000 bees in a hive, most of which are female *worker bees*. Several hundred male bees, called d*rones*, live in the hive until they are needed to mate with a new queen from another hive.

Flowers secrete a sweet liquid, called *nectar*, to attract bees, who gather *pollen* as they sip the nectar. The bees brush the pollen against the female part of a blossom so that it produces seeds, fruit, or vegetables. This is called *pollination*. Much of the food we eat has to be pollinated by bees in order to grow.

Bees eat nectar for its sugar, and they eat pollen for its protein. Worker bees take nectar back to the hive, where they fan it with their wings to thicken it into honey, which is the hive's food during the winter. They do a special dance to direct other workers to flowers with lots of pollen or nectar.

Bees communicate by *pheromones*, or smells. When Aunt Celine "smoked" the hive on the roof of Lionel's apartment building, she masked the smell so the bees couldn't communicate the "alarm" pheromone. That made it possible for her to handle the *frames* in the hive, as we see her doing in the illustration, without being stung.

Beekeeping and honey collection date back 4,000 years. Honey never spoils, and it is the only food that contains all the substances necessary to sustain life. Honeybees were carried across the Atlantic Ocean to North America by the Pilgrims to pollinate their apple trees. Before that there were other pollinating insects in North America, but not honeybees.

Honeybee populations are declining throughout North America and in Europe. The possible causes include pesticides, a loss of plant diversity due to monoculture, and a parasitic mite called the varroa, which burrows into young bees and feeds on them. Concern about this decline has led to a resurgence of urban beekeeping in cities across Europe and America. Washington, D.C., New York, Los Angeles, and Philadelphia are among the American cities that are buzzing with bees.

There are hundreds of hives in Paris—in public parks, on the roofs of famous buildings, on apartment balconies. Like Lionel and Aunt Celine, Paris's *apiculteurs*, or beekeepers, have discovered that honeybees are happier in the city than in the surrounding countryside. Paris allows no pesticides or fertilizers, it hosts a great diversity of flowering trees and plants, and—like cities everywhere—it is warmer than the surrounding countryside, which means that plants are in bloom longer. Beehives in Paris produce three to five times as much honey as hives in the nearby countryside!

The daughter of Hungarian immigrants to America, ANDREA CHENG (1957–2015) married a son of Chinese immigrants, and her children's books reflect her multicultural roots. These include the picture book *Grandfather Counts*, the YA novel *Marika*, the middle-grade story *The Lace Dowry*, her Anna Wang novels, and others. Tilbury House published her picture book *When the Bees Fly Home* in 2002, and Andrea remained fascinated by bees throughout her life.

SARAH MCMENEMY (London, England) has illustrated several bestselling children's books including *Waggle*, *Jack's New Boat*, and *Everybody Bonjours!* A permanent public display of her art graces rail station platforms in London's East End. She studied illustration in England and America and works internationally. Sarah holds great affection for Paris, where she lived for a time.

Tilbury House Publishers
12 Starr Street
Thomaston, Maine 04861
800-582-1899 • www.tilburyhouse.com

Text © 2017 by Andrea Cheng
Illustrations © 2017 by Sarah McMenemy

Hardcover ISBN 978-088448-520-9
eBook ISBN 978-9-88448-599-5

First hardcover printing October 2017

15 16 17 18 19 20 XXX 10 9 8 7 6 5 4 3 2 1

Library of Congress Control Number: 2017937853

Cover and text designed by Lemniscates Studio, Barcelona, Spain
Printed in China through Four Colour Print Group, Louisville, KY